Penelope's Headache
(Tattle or Tell)

Cindy Goldberg

Illustrations by Rina Risnawati

ISBN-13: 978-1519196439

Dedicated to Dale, Becka and Erika

Penelope came home at ten past three,
she let herself in with a brand new key.
Pouring herself a glass to drink,
she sat right down so she could think.

Her mom came in the room soon after,
expecting to hear Penny's bright laughter.
Instead Penny's eyes were shut tight,
it was clear to mom that something was not right.

"Sweetie, what's wrong?" were the first words she said,
"I don't know mom, there's so many thoughts in my head."
Miss Nora said we should not tattle, to get kids in trouble
except when there's danger, then we must tell on the double!

"I cannot figure out just what to do,
when do I tell and then again, who?"
"I am all mixed up between tattling and telling,
that my head hurts so bad and my brain may be swelling."

"Okay, said mom, what is it that's confusing you?
I know this is complicated, although very true.
Knowing the difference between tattle and tell,
even at my age won't always work well."

"Well mom. This happened today,
Ryan fell because Zack ran past him to play.
Zackary looked and saw that Ryan was fine,
but he did not help and just got into line.
Mom, what Zack did was not very nice,
should I have told on him, what's your advice?

You are right to be concerned about Ryan,
it sounds like Zack stopped and there was no crying.
I think it all worked out pretty well,
you should not worry, you were right not to tell.

Thanks mom, but there was another,
Cara gets hit hard by her big brother.
She's scared to go home and showed me her bruise,
her brother is fifteen, how do I choose?

This time Cara could get hurt far worse,
you should tell me, your teacher, counselor or nurse.
When a friend may be in any danger at all,
you must tell a grown-up. That's the right call.

This is helping me mom, but there's more in my head,
Jenny threw an eraser when Miss Nora turned her head.
Miss Nora did not know who did that bad thing,
I wanted to tell on Jenny but then I heard the bell ring.

It sounds like your teacher did not ask,
telling on Jenny was not your task.
If no one was hurt or bullied at all,
that would be tattling, you made the right call.

My head feels less crowded, but there still is one more,
I watched this happen and felt sick to my core.
Tim was on the playground playing alone,
some big kids said, move or we'll break all your bones.

Tim walked away looking scared and so sad,
I wanted to tell someone quite awfully bad.

Penelope dear, you knew what to do,
that sounds like a case of bullying too.
Whenever you see someone threatened or harmed,
telling is the right choice, let that be your alarm.

Penelope I think you know,
when to tell and when to go.
If someone is scared, hurt or upset,
because something bad has happened or may yet,
you should tell and you will aid
a child who is hurt or very afraid.

You know what I think, Penelope dear,
this can be easy and it can be clear.
If someone is hurt or you know that they might,
telling is your job to make things right!

If someone in your class breaks a rule,
like budging or talking or acting like a fool,
the child may be silly or not behaving well,
that's when it's tattling so you should NOT tell.

Getting them in trouble is not your place,
that is the time when you stay in your space.

Follow your heart because soon you will know,
when to tell an adult and when to let it go.

Penelope and mom settled right in,
to homework and dinner and being tucked in.
Penelope's brain was no longer swelling,
she now knows the difference between tattling and telling.

Note to Teachers and Parents

Tattling vs. Telling is a dilemma in the minds of elementary age children. The decision making process needs to be taught by caring adults who can convey that it is always best to tell an adult when someone is hurt, may get hurt, has been bullied, is sick, scared and/or when a child is in any type of danger. On the other hand tattling to get another child in trouble should be discouraged.

Penelope's Headache is the starting place for an ongoing discussion in the Tattling vs. Telling learning process.

A variety of situations may be presented to children in a classroom or at home after reading and discussing this book. Identifying situations that require telling an adult vs. tattling is one way to teach this valuable social skill.

For your convenience, enlarge and copy the table on the next page. Cut each section out. Use the situations to discuss whether tattling or telling is the right response.

What Should You Do if you See…

A child is hitting another child.	A child put a library book on the wrong shelf.	A child fell, got up and brushed herself off.	A child is lying on the ground crying.	A child "budged" in line.	A child told you that she stole someone's lunch money.
A child told you that he didn't do his homework.	A child is bleeding.	A child used inappropriate language.	An adult hit a child.	A child accidentally bumped into another child.	A child sticks her tongue out at another child.
A child was running in the halls.	A child is throwing up in the bathroom.	A child was climbing over the bathroom stall.	Your best friend is upset with you.	You had an argument with a child.	A child fell off of the monkey bars and is on the ground.

Tattle or Tell Brainstorming

Telling an adult is important when someone is in danger, is hurt or may be in danger.

Tattling is used to get someone in trouble.

Brainstorm a list of situations that happen in your class/home with your child/class. Use the chart on the following page to list situations that belong in the tattle column and those that belong in the tell column.

Tattle | Tell

ACKNOWLEDGMENTS

Thanks to all of my students for needing this story to help them with an important decision. Thanks to Helen Ward for her honesty and support.

Made in the USA
Middletown, DE
26 August 2018